GUT FEELINGS

FROSTBITE, MAGGOTS, MENINGITIS AND MORE ...
TRUSTING YOUR INTUITION IN MEDICAL MOMENTS
THAT MATTER FROM THE NORTH POLE
TO THE EQUATOR

Dr. Fizzy Lillingston

Foreword by Sir Ranulph Fiennes; Explorer

Gut Feelings
Frostbite, Maggots, Meningitis and more ...
Trusting your intuition in medical moments that matter
from the North Pole to the equator.
Lillingston, Felicity (Fizzy)

Copyright © 2019 by Felicity Lillingston (Fizzy)

ISBN: 978-1698849676

All right reserved by the author, including the right to reproduce this book or portions thereof in any form whatsoever. No part of this publication may be reproduced, stored in a retrieval system or transmitted in any form or by any means, electronic, mechanical, photography, recording, scanning or otherwise.

The medical and health stories in this book are purely for interest and entertainment only and should not be used for any diagnostic or treatment purposes. All the stories in this book are taken from true life experiences and as such are from the memory of the author and not taken from any other manuscript or hearsay.

The author and publisher expressly disclaim all responsibility and shall have no liability, for any damages, loss or injury, or liability whatsoever as a result of information obtained in this book. Neither the author nor the publisher endorses any test, treatment or procedure mentioned in this book or accompanying website.

Please consult your own health care provider before making any healthcare decisions or for guidance about specific medical conditions.

Published by:
10-10-10 Publishing
Markham, Ontario

First 10-10-10 Publishing paperback edition October

Contents

That Gut Feeling	v
Dedication	vii
Foreword	ix
Acknowledgements	xi
Introduction	xvii
Chapter 1: Polar Bear Encounter - It's Behind You!	1
Chapter 2: Meningitis - A Close Shave!	11
Chapter 3: Bad Air - Early Expedition Shock?	17
Chapter 4: Chainsaw Trauma - Do We Remove Or Not?	27
Chapter 5: Arctic Blizzard - Mission Medical Log ....Critical!	35
Chapter 6: Psychotic Attack - Never Turn Your Back!	43
Chapter 7: Flesh-Eating Disease - 1575 MEDEVAC Miles Away	49
Chapter 8: Her Dazzle - Just Naturally with Gravity !	57
Chapter 9: Maggots and Spiders - Wildlife in Unexpected Places!	63
Chapter 10: The Little Caribbean Miracle - Spontaneous Healing?	73
About the Author	79

That *Gut* Feeling

This book contains a collection of short stories from a clinical perspective, from my time as a nurse, expedition medic and now a doctor. An eclectic series of experiences after 40 years in practice.

These stories are taken from my time as the medic on two Arctic expeditions, from clinical practice in the United Kingdom, around the world, and on humanitarian projects. They describe some of those unexpected clinical moments including life-threatening medical emergencies.

Fizzy Lillingston

"How strange is the lot of us mortals! Each of us is here for a brief sojourn; for what purpose he knows not, though he sometimes thinks he senses it. But without deeper reflection one knows from daily life that one exists for other people - first of all for all those upon whose smiles and well being our own happiness is wholly dependent, and then for the many unknown to us, to whose destinies we are bound by the ties of sympathy."
Albert Einstein

I dedicate this book to all those seeking to explore the unknown and take a jump into the great adventure, which is our amazing lives.

Be open to the wonderful possibilities in your life and turn them into magical actualities. Don't dither on the edge of maybe, just jump right in and do it!

Fizzy Lillingston

You miss 100% of the shots you don't take
(Wayne Gretzky)

Foreword

I was first in contact with Fizzy Lillingston and her team in 2003 when I agreed to advise on an Arctic expedition, where she was the medical officer.

As any explorer is aware, being part of a team is paramount when considering survival. Her team had been selected carefully, and after a considerable selection process they were picked for not only their *guts* but also their keenness to work together, to support each other. All of this, in one of the most inhospitable parts of the world, where survival reverts back to human instinct, and often depends on an immediate *gut* reaction.

As the patron for the expedition and having spent much of my life exploring inhospitable parts of the world, I can verify it takes care to go where Mother Nature does not make you welcome. Trying to survive in -40 °C day and night for over a month in the Arctic, with none of the creature comforts that we take for granted in our everyday lives, is not everyone's cup of tea! To be the medical officer for any Arctic expedition is a responsibility not to be taken lightly. Anything could happen to any one of the team while exploring many hundreds of miles away from civilization. This is undoubtedly where that *gut feeling* matters and can be the difference between life and death!

Gut Feelings

This book is written by a gutsy lady who has put together a clever eclectic collection of *gut* reactions of various sorts, and not just from her Arctic experiences.

I encourage you to read this book to take a journey into the world of *Gut Feelings* to enjoy the stories which come from various parts of the world, where Fizzy has travelled, including the North Pole. Be prepared to be shocked, amazed and downright horrified by some of the stories.

Enjoy
Ranulph Fiennes

Acknowledgements

With deepest gratitude to:
The Ice Warrior Expedition for enabling me to experience a life-changing Arctic adventure.

To its founder **Jim McNeil** for his dream, and for allowing his team to be a part of this.

To the other members of the Geomagnetic North Pole team who shared those special moments where no words were necessary to explain the despair of the constant cold and trying to survive and reach our goal. Thank you for that group hug at the beginning of every day when things looked impossible - these kept us sane! Thank you **Julia, Dave, Matt and Mark** - you did and always will have a special place in my heart.

To Sir **Ranulph Fiennes**, our patron for the Arctic expeditions and one of the greatest explorers of our time. You have been my life-long inspiration for showing me how determination, hard work and never giving up is the way to achieve what you really want in life! I don't think I would have volunteered for the North Pole expedition had I not read about your adventures. Your inspiring expeditions gave me that tingling *gut* excitement to go beyond my comfort zone, and fueled my interest in exploring.

Thank you as well, Ran, for writing my foreword!

To all my tutors at St Bartholomew's Hospital, London where I learnt a lot of life's important lessons. Mainly, the best is the only way; doing something only partially well is not the 'Bart's way'! Using this teaching throughout my life has reaped rewards beyond belief.

To my father, who taught me to learn wisdom and be proud of it. To reach the top and to be a 'Mighty Mouse' (his nickname for me) in a big world. Without his constant expectations, I would never have been driven to acquire those gifts that were waiting for me. He always encouraged me to be sensitive to others' needs. I'll never forget seeing him crying on Remembrance Day when he recapped the memory of losing a dear friend who stood beside him on the bridge of a boat when it was bombed during the Second World War. He survived unharmed while his friend received a direct hit.

To my mother, whose untimely death when I was 15 left me with a hole that was hard to fill. My wonderful family have helped here, especially my daughter whose humanitarian work in Africa is following the work her grandmother did out there, all those years ago.

To **Dr Guy Bullen**, my brother, who always made life an adventure, especially when we were children. You inspired me to be different, climb those trees and as a result enabled me to stand on my own two feet. I'm still climbing Guy!

To **Raymond Aaron** and his team for encouraging me along the route to becoming an author. Without their inspiration, this book may always have been just a pipe dream.

To all my students at St George's University, whose enthusiasm and incredible resilience has given me faith in those current aspiring medical and vet students. Their dreams and aspirations gave me reassurance that our future doctors and vets will be enlightened and awesome!

To **Dr Randal Waechter** for his undying enthusiasm and support; a true mentor in the research field. His encouragement led to my first publication.

To **Dr Paul Fields, Dr Callum Macpherson**, and all the staff at The Windwards Islands Research Institute for your support and belief in all I was trying to achieve.

To all my patients during my 42 years of being in the caring profession, you have taught me to listen to my *gut!*

To **Dame Jean Robinson** for allowing me to be part of The Children's Health Organisation Relief and Educational Services (CHORES) and experience the amazing humanitarian work that is being done on the Island of Grenada.

To **Sue Field,** whose enthusiasm for learning and discovering new boundaries was and still is a constant inspiration.

Gut Feelings

To all my sailing chums who've shared our adventures on the high seas. A special thanks to all those who worked tirelessly to help with aid for those trying to survive on the stricken Island of Dominica following the devastation wrought by hurricane Maria.

To all my wonderful friends who have given me inspiration, encouragement and support throughout my life. Especially **Eugénie Griffths, Clare Thomas, Di Leal, Sue Harris, Celia** and **Stephen Johnstone, Sheridan** and **David Steen, Jane** and **Johny Chadd, Debbie** and **David Sprake, Jane** and **Peter Cazalet, Nikki** and **Charles Wright, Gracie Wright, Karen** and **Charlie Hopkins, Gail** and **Tim Evans, Carla Gregory** and **Alex Helbig, John ('The Dean')** and **Gill Douch, Linda Melton** and **Ian Park, Sarah** and **Darrel Barnes, Rachel** and **Chris Morejohn Platt, Dick** and **Anita Johnson, Vanessa Biddulph** and **Bill Oakes, Lindsay** and **Tina Clubb, Jane Famous, Fran Smith, Wendy** and **Jim Francis, Jackie Furgeson, Susie Hayward, Lizzie** and **Paul Hyde, Jojo** and **Simon Pickering Pullman, Robin Toozs-Hobson, Jyoti Amarnani, Wendy** and **Ian Hines.** Ashley and **Steve Mcphee.** Jenny Allen and her **pig, Bob** and **Mina Linley, Vanessa** and **Gary Haynes, Sam,Ed** and **Harry Toms, Caroline Ogilvie, Sandra Hurlock, Jackie** and **David Pugh.** Mandie Steel, John Louis Davy, Stella and **John Dyer, Andrew** and **Inga Weston, Susie Stanthorp, Bill Warburg, Caroline** and **Peter Hambley, Lynn Williams,** Sarah and **David Howieson, Susi** and **Hank Koorstra, Chris** and **Sharon Mildenhall, Joany** and **Graham, Graham Beaumont, Guy Draper, Robert Sladden, Jemima Tindle, Gwen Burbank, Hans Peter Maresch** and **Doris Kote Dr**

Gut Feelings

Susan Anne Bretherto, Hugh Heron, Hallie Tamez, Jane and **Michael Barraclough, Mark** and **Sandy Donald, Sarah** and **Dennis Passingham, Jenny** and **Simon Wilmshurst, Jamie** and **Jenny MacAlister, Emma Reuss, Paul Moss, Dr Richard Amerling, Elizabeth Anne Buck, Scott Watson, Irene Barkley, Bill Warburg, Charles** and **Susie Deakin, Christopher Langley, Nicole Rambau.** And so many more people I have met along the way - thank you for being there for me.

To all my long-suffering family including my amazing children, **Tori, Ant** and **Pete,** who have been the source of so much emotion, love, gratitude and just downright pride! You have taught me how to experience unimaginable love and joy, and to learn patience and trust. You are my life, my loves, my past, present and my future.

To my husband **Jack** whose never-ending support has been behind me throughout our 40 years of marriage. You have always been encouraging in all my mad endeavors, including allowing me to risk life and limb and walk to the North Pole. Without your constant backing, I would not be where I am today. It is your patience, steadfast belief and love that have enabled me to achieve all I have. Thank you for encouraging me to write this book. My gratitude is beyond words.

Introduction

That *Gut* feeling
Intuition - to break it down - *in tuition* - *your inner you, tutoring you!*

I've learnt to appreciate my *gut* feelings/intuition over my 40 years in clinical practice.

I've had the privilege, in health care, of being a part of others' lives at times of great difficulty and vulnerability.

When I get that *gut* feeling that something isn't right about a patient or the situation they are in, I trust it. This has not been taught; however, years of experiencing patients in extreme situations have taught me to listen to that *gut* instinct and act on it.

Researchers have found evidence that people can use their intuition to make faster and more accurate decisions. A professor at the University of New South Wales in Australia and lead author of the study done in 2016 found that intuition can be measured and does exist.

His findings support the notion that non-conscious emotion can bias non-emotional behaviour - a process of intuition. (*http://www2.psy.unsw.edu.au/Users/CDonkin/publications/psci16.pdf*)

Science is beginning to recognise the reality of intuition, how natural it is and where it comes from. So if you're thinking that intuition has nothing to do with intelligence, then you're not alone. It is such a difficult thing to observe and measure. It has been described as *"the ability to understand something immediately, without the need for conscious reasoning."*

The Merriam-Webster dictionary describes it as *"a natural or inherent aptitude or impulse, or capacity that is mediated by reactions below the conscious level."*

Steve Jobs is quoted as saying that *"Intuition is absolutely more powerful than intellect."*

In other words, intuition is our first instinct, right away before the mind has consciously analysed the situation. Throughout history there have been anecdotal reports of people surviving near death experiences by pure instinct, especially at times where there is no time to critically analyse the situation or weigh the pros and cons.

So where does it come from? Most people can recognise that feeling in their gut when something just doesn't feel right. Some people say they feel it in their heart and the heart reacts before

Introduction

the mind.

Forbes calls intuition *"the highest form of intelligence"* and Geird Gigerenzer, a German psychologist, and one of the directors of the Max Plank Institute for Human Development, claims that the intelligence of the unconscious is both *"intuitive and rational"*. He has studied the use of bounded rationality and heuristics in decision making and argues, intuition is less about *"suddenly knowing"* the answer but more about instinctively understanding what information is unimportant and can be discarded.

Throughout my clinical practice, I have always wondered when I'm diagnosing a patient's condition, how I know immediately when someone is what we call 'big sick' as opposed to just 'under the weather'.

Wikipedia suggest - I quote:

"a diagnosis is based on laboratory reports or test results, rather than the physical examination of the patient." They do go onto explain, however that a full diagnosis for an infectious disease usually requires both an examination for signs and symptoms and laboratory checks.

The Mayo Clinic gives this advice to their patients. A diagnosis may be drawn from 3 things -

1. A physical examination

2. A lab test
3. A psychological evaluation

Without these further tests it is interesting to surmise how a clinician knows if urgent action should be taken *now*, or if they can wait for the lab results. Sometimes it's blatantly obvious; however, often in the early stages, it's just not (see chapter 2). In my experience one has a hunch/ instinct that something is very wrong.

Many words come to mind when thinking about how one comes to an initial impression of a possible diagnosis. These include clinical experiences, presenting symptoms, intuition, *gut* feelings and just the plain obvious. However, during my 40 years of clinical practice, I believe it is all of these. I often liken a presenting case to a detective looking at all the evidence, with the hopeful result of drawing an accurate conclusion and finding the culprit.

We all dread missing that one piece of evidence that would have led us to the correct diagnosis.

'Never leave any stone unturned' is my motto when looking at a presenting case.

This reminds me of a scenario which on first observation led me quickly down the line to 'meningitis' or some other serious blood complaint. The child presented with multiple purple, none fading, marks to his body, legs and arms. This, however, turned out, on further in-depth questioning, to be the result of playing in a children's ball play park all day the preceding day. The child had spent a good deal of the previous day rolling about and jumping in and out of a large area filled with small rubber balls! Bouncing among these small balls had led to multiple mini bruises to his whole body.

The resultant exhaustion and bruising over the entire body was as a direct result of *having a jolly good time!* Mum was suitably reassured and red flags and worsening advice were given in case there was to be any deterioration in the child's health.

As stated by Arthur Colan Doyle in his Sherlock Holmes series: "When you have eliminated the impossible, whatever remains, however impossible, must be the truth."

It is worth noting that the *gut* is also the home to trillions of living organisms from bacteria, microbiota, fungi archaea and protozoans. These can affect every part of your body, from your brain to your mind. It is now being understood that this biodiversity can affect, not only the immune system, but also one's feelings. A new study done on two large European groups found that certain species of bacteria were missing in people with depression. The *gut* after all has its own nervous system, the enteric nervous system, so if something happens in the *gut*/digestive tract then it naturally can affect the mood.

There is a lot more to your *gut* than at first meets the eye! It's even been suggested that ones attempts at weight loss can be affected by the personal micro biome in the gut.

So, that *gut feeling i*s more than just a feeling!

I hope you enjoy this short collection of a few of my life experiences when I had those *gut* feelings!

Chapter 1
Polar Bear Encounter - It's Behind You!

> *"Whoever has experienced near-death,*
> *knows how gracious it is to be alive."*
> — Lailah Gifty Akita

As the medical officer on an Arctic expedition to the Geomagnetic North Pole, it was my responsibility to check the other 5 team members daily for any bruising, frostbite and other ailments that presented after trekking all day.

We were two weeks into the expedition and we were all settling down for the evening.

We had just set up camp and were getting the stoves alight to melt the snow for our reconstituted dried food rations. The team was in the tent and I had gone out to my sled (pulk) for some medical supplies. I was looking for various dressings and in particular a tube of antibacterial cream. As I rummaged about, I began to feel a deep creeping primeval *gut* feeling of fear. A feeling that I was being watched. I stood up and slowly turned around, fingering my pepper spray in my pocket as I scanned the horizon for any signs of a polar bear. All the time remembering that I was definitely not at the top of the pecking order out there where polar bears ruled the roost. They are known to be the largest carnivore (meat eater) that lives on land.

During the expedition, we had seen quite a few polar bear footprints but never an actual bear.

We kept a keen look out while trekking and always changed the team member at the back of the trek line every hour. It was their responsibility to keep a checkout behind.

Polar bears do not tend to hunt humans; in fact they are easily scared off when confronted. They feed mainly on seals. They have, however, been known to attack humans when they feel threatened or if they are extremely hungry. We were all well aware that most people attacked by a polar bear do not survive. Polar bears are not only extremely big and strong, but are also very instinctive, and once they have fresh meat available, they are very difficult to ward off.

The whole team was trained prior to the expedition in handling firearms. Lying ready on top of the last pulk (sled) at the rear of the expedition was a rifle, primed and ready should a polar bear attack. We all had a pepper spray in an outside pocket and flares which when fired, we were reliably informed, were a good polar bear deterrent. Unlike brown bears, polar bears are not territorial. Although often perceived as being voraciously aggressive, polar bears are normally cautious in confrontations, and often choose to escape rather than fight, unless of course they are starving.

To kill a polar bear would naturally be our last resort; we were aware that in an extreme situation we might have to use the rifle. In Northern Canada and the High Arctic, where the majority of polar bears are to be found, they are now on the list of endangered animals. This area is home to nearly two-thirds of the world's estimated 25,000 remaining polar bears. They are hunted both for their meat and for their thick, furry white pelts. The Northern Canada has a legal and scientifically managed polar bear hunting protocol and only Inuit and trophy hunters guided by an Inuit can hunt polar bears. So if we were to shoot and kill a polar bear it would be purely in self-defence, and only happen after having tried every other method first.

We had woken the previous morning to find the tent surrounded by polar bear prints. It looked like only one set, but our nocturnal visitor had circumnavigated the tent a couple of times. The prints looked big and were a reminder that we were not alone out here and an easy target for a hungry bear. As we slept he could easily have ripped open our fragile tent. There was not much between an 8ft hungry polar bear, a tent canvas and 6 tasty humans!

That evening I was on my own outside the tent, gathering medical supplies from my pulk, when I started to feel that I was not alone.

I scanned the horizon; polar bears have white fur as a camouflage in their environment. It is therefore extremely difficult to see them against the never-ending white Arctic background. It is interesting to note that polar bears in fact have black skin, and the reason they look white is because the hairs are hollow and have no white pigment at all.

As I scanned the Arctic wastes, I couldn't see any reason for my *gut* feelings of discomfort. The coast seemed to be clear. Nothing was moving in the vast expanse of white snow that surrounded me. I returned to the task at hand and carried on getting the dressings and medical supplies out. My hands were full so I placed the tube of cream to hold in my mouth while I carried on searching. Unfortunately the tube had metal in it and it froze firmly to my lips. As I was gently trying to persuade the tube to let go of my lips, I saw something moving in my peripheral vision. It was then that my primitive *gut* went into overdrive as the nauseating realisation dawned on me that I was very close to an 8ft killing machine and my life was in serious danger!

To my horror, an extremely large polar bear stood up from behind our tent and started advancing as he sniffed the air. In the back of my mind a flash reminder came to me that a hunting polar bear can run up to 40kms an hour. I would not have a chance should he choose to attack.

We eyeballed each other and I nearly passed out! I remember going through all the things not to do if you encounter a polar bear.

- Do not run
- Do not behave like prey
- Do act like a threat
- Do use the pepper spray

As my life passed before me I tried to call the team in the tent; however, as you may remember, I had placed a metal tube of cream between my lips which meant shouting out was extremely difficult. To rip the tube from my lips would make them bleed and I was well aware that I was facing an instinctive beast who, when he smelt blood, wouldn't think twice about attacking! I managed a muffled desperate yelp for help to the others who were huddled around a noisy cooking stove in the tent and unlikely to hear me.

It is extraordinary how at times like this one finds time to think of family and friends at home that you may never see again.

As the polar bear went down onto his all fours he started rocking from side to side and as his ears were back I knew he was preparing to pounce. *This is it*, I thought, and almost fainted!

At that very moment, to my immense relief, the tent flap opened and one of the team popped his head out to see how why I was taking so long. He took one look at my horror struck frozen face and saw my pointing finger. He quickly grabbed the rifle and as he came out of the tent, let off a shot into the air. He was closely followed by the others with flares at the ready. They were all making as much noise as possible to scare the bear off.

Unfortunately the rifle shots did nothing to stop the oncoming polar bear. In retrospect the sound of a gunshot is very similar to the noise of the ice cracking, which was a regular noise out there on the sea ice as the tides shift in the ocean below. Due to the ongoing and potential loss of their sea ice habitat, as a result of climate change, polar bears have been listed as a threatened species under the Endangered Species Act of May 2008, so we were all fully aware and sensitive to the fact that shooting one would be as a last resort and only if there was a threat to life.

As the bear continued to advance, our desperate marksman was considering a rifle shot to his body, when one of the other team members let off a flare. The first flare unfortunately landed behind the polar bear, driving him forward.

Noooooooooooo !!!!

A second flare was deployed and happily made its mark and fell at his feet. This thankfully stopped him dead in his tracks. He hesitated, looked confused and then looking disconcerted he slowly turned and lumbered off, every now and again turning to look our way.

As we watched him go we noticed he was quite dirty and very thin and looked extremely hungry. We presumed he was probably a young male who was down on his luck. Unhappily for us as he would probably not give up now he'd smelt the potential of 6 tasty snacks!

That night we not only slept in a huddle in the middle of the tent away from the canvas edge, but we also rigged up a booby trap around the tent. We strung a rope from our skis around the tent and hung saucepans and boots on it. This we hoped would not only deter him but also warn us should he return.

It took a very long time for a very shaken team to return to any feeling of normality again.

We were all extremely affected by the encounter and very relieved to have survived. We were grateful to be alive.

Chapter 2
Meningitis - A Close Shave!

"Peace is the beauty of life. It is sunshine. It is the smile of a child, the love of a mother, the joy of a father, the togetherness of a family. It is the advancement of man, the victory of a just cause, the triumph of truth."
— Menachem Begin

It was another busy day in an Out of Hours GP Urgent Care Shift. During this clinical shift, we saw patients who would generally consult their GP during the day. If, however, they fell ill unexpectedly after their GP clinic closed, then they could access the OOH service. We saw all sorts of medical issues, which as a general rule, were not very urgent and could easily wait until the following day; however, one could never tell, as this case will illustrate.

I was beginning to flag after seeing my 15th viral upper respiratory tract infection (common cold) that just needed reassurance and over the counter symptoms control.

The government awareness campaigns recently widely advertised, regarding treating the common cold at home, just didn't seem to be getting through.

My next patient seemed on the surface to be just another worried mum with her 10 month old son. As a routine with every patient, I take a full history and did the usual full and thorough top to toe examination. The child was awake and compliant to all of my full body examination. He seemed calm and quiet, and afterwards sat quietly in his buggy. Mum reported that it was probably nothing; however, little Johnny (not his real name) had not been himself for the last 24 hours. He was playing with his food and not keen to drink much. I agreed that this was nothing unusual with any child at the onset of any viral infection.

I reassured her that the full examination was unremarkable, apart from a very mild pyrexia (temperature).

At this stage in the consultation, I would usually go on to discuss what we call red flags and advise mum when to contact further urgent care services should his condition worsen or he developed any new and worrying symptoms. I would carry on to offer advice on home care and which over the counter medication from the pharmacy she could use for symptom relief.

For some reason, however, my voice faltered and I was unable to discharge this patient with this advice - I had this *gut* feeling that all was not well here. I had noticed that, when following my commands, little Johnny was ever so slightly delayed in his responses. Mum said he was a slow and steady child and although a little less active today, this was not unusual for him when he was tired or unwell.

Meningitis - A Close Shave!

I was not convinced by her comments which did nothing to reassure my *gut* feeling. I heard myself saying that although I could find nothing to worry about when I'd carried out my examination, I was nonetheless going to get a second opinion.

So I followed my *gut* instinct and referred the child to the on call pediatric team at the local hospital. This was not an easy referral as I had no clear reason for my referral apart from my *gut* feelings. Happily the receiving on call team was willing to see the child for a further assessment.

I then continued my shift and went home. The case of this child, however, continued to nag at me and the following day I rang the pediatric team to see if they had kept the child in. I was passed on to the Senior House Officer who was keen to speak to the referring clinician. She asked me directly, how did I know? Know what, I replied? Little Johnny apparently had early onset meningitis and was almost symptomless when I saw him. Within 3 hours the child had deteriorated so fast that he was now fighting for his life in the special care baby unit with full blown meningitis. I was taken aback. If I had sent the child home with worsening symptoms advice, as his presenting symptoms suggested, the child may not have received the care he needed when he did and may well have died!

How did I know? - There was consciously nothing in his examination that indicated meningitis apart for a very mild temperature, similar in fact to many of the other cases I had seen that day.

What made me refer this child to secondary care?

I'll never know, apart from that *gut* feeling that led me to subconsciously know that this was not another upper respiratory infection and that this child was in fact just about to be '*big sick*'. I was humbled by this case, and my practice was enriched by such inner tuition.

Happily little Johnny made a full recovery. I was reunited with them 4 weeks later when mum brought him in to see me. I still have mum's note of thanks. One of those special moments that one will never forget and that make ones job so special and rewarding.

Chapter 3
Bad Air - Early Expedition Shock?

"He lives most life whoever breathes most air."
— Elizabeth Barrett Browning

In 2004 a team of 6 amateur explorers set out on an expedition to the Geomagnetic North Pole. I was the medical officer on the expedition. The unsupported 340 mile walk to the Geomagnetic North Pole was by foot pulling our sleds (pulks). These sleds carried enough supplies to last us for the whole expedition, as well as many medical supplies deemed necessary for an unsupported expedition.

With the unlikelihood of immediate rescue, being many hundreds of miles away from civilisation, I was well equipped for most emergencies. It was my job to make sure my team was well and fit for the task ahead. I was fully aware of the fragility of our situation on the sea ice, having spent three months the previous year dealing with various medical situations. In fact, on another expedition just before we left, we heard of a member of their team who had fallen through the sea ice just the week before, with the result of full body frostbite, hypothermia and subsequent death. I was, by now, well aware that this was not a hospitable place to be practicing medicine!

I had a great team, however, who were fit, both mentally and physically. We had done a lot of training and preparing together whilst also raising money and awareness for cancer research. Our team leader was organised and competent.

The first medical emergency, unexpectedly happened after only about 8 hours on the ice and was a shock to us all.

Our first step of the expedition was to fly by Twin Otter plane, north east 628km from Resolute Bay to Eureka weather station over the desolate sea ice. Eureka weather station is a bleak place and the furthest habitable spot before arctic wastes. It was the starting point for our 340 mile trek. The weather station is manned by one lonely soul who does 3 months in his post alone before he gets relieved. He was, as a result, delighted by our unexpected visit and gave an enthusiastic welcome, brandishing his camera. I don't think many people drop by during his watch, apart from mad explorers and the odd Inuit hunting with dog sleds.

Once we were dropped off by the Twin Otter, we watched the plane slowly disappear over the horizon and suddenly felt very alone. We were excited to be setting off at last; however, we were also in awe of the task ahead. Our bodies and minds had been trained and we were keen to set off together to explore what lay ahead. As we set off up Eureka Sound the temperature was around -40 °C, and with the wind chill it felt considerably colder. It was a desolate spot where there were few living creatures. The sea ice stretched out white before us for miles and miles, with wedges of sea ice and ice rubble as far as you could see. We set off walking on the sea ice up Eureka Sound. During the summer, the tides below cause the sea ice to move and crack and throw the sea up into ever bigger and bigger piles of ice rubble. These were a struggle to climb over dragging a 90kg sledge behind one. It was soon made clear to us that we were there by our own insistence and not by invitation. The Arctic is a hostile place where man is not meant to survive.

We had spent time acclimatising at base camp in Resolute while waiting for a good weather window to set off, so we were somewhat prepared for the extreme temperatures. It was however much colder than we had expected and we didn't walk far on the first evening as we were keen to get our tent up and get our stoves going before the temperature fell further. With the wind chill this would fall even more and be almost untenable for life!

This extreme cold made it hard to breathe, and the moisture which we take for granted when we breathe in a warm climate froze on our faces and in our nasal passages. Any hair on the face, in your nose, beard, moustache, eyebrows and even eyelashes froze and crackled when one blinked. One tried to breathe slowly to warm the air as it came in, but this was not easy when struggling to pull a sled over mountains of sea ice rubble. The pulks always came back at one on the downward movement and hit one in the back, calves and even head! Within minutes on the ice the pulks were named. You F... ing B.......or you Sh.. or frankly words I won't repeat. Bruised and battered we soon decided to make camp early that first night and lick our wounds. It was always important to keep moving and we all worked as fast as possible to put up the tent for our first night on the sea ice. We had planned to put up two tents; however, the extreme cold and effort to erect even one in less than -40 °C temperatures meant that we plumped for one. The sealed tent was duly erected, but slowly - it's interesting how one slows down in the extreme cold. On our previous research expedition, where I was collecting blood samples, we had discovered the effect of extreme cold on the hormone thyroxine and the bodies' hormone economy response to extreme cold which slows one down considerably. We were aware of this; it meant, though, that we took a lot longer setting up the tent and performing activities than we had when preparing for the expedition in warmer climates.

We then collected snow to melt in saucepans on our stoves, using the water to rehydrate our expedition food and for drinking. We did not carry water but relied on melting the snow lying on top of the sea ice.

Lighting the stoves was an interesting procedure as most fuel freezes at -20 °C . This meant that between us we had to warm up the fuel to above -20 °C before we could get it to ignite. We actioned this by stuffing the fuel can down inside our jackets and walking about with it before we passed it onto the next in line, like some sort of weird relay race.

After a frustrating 30 minutes and far too many used matches, we all cheered as the stove burst into action. We then settled down in the tent in the hope of some moderate lifting of the extreme temperatures.

Bad Air - Early Expedition Shock?

After a while, however, one after the other, we all started to feel extremely unwell with nausea, headaches, extreme weakness, dizziness, shortness of breath, confusion, blurred vision and eventually collapse.

What was going on??

That *gut* feeling came to me that our lives were in extreme danger; *"Let's get out of here ASAP."*

The air was bad!

We evacuated from the tent, and fell onto the sea ice in various stages of delirium, confusion and collapse. This was not a good condition to be in at - 40 °C and lowering further temperatures as the wind chill picked up. To be immobilised and confused lying out on the sea ice was a serious threat to life in those conditions.

What had happened? We all looked as if we had been poisoned. And indeed we had; we were all suffering from acute carbon monoxide poisoning!

I knew that following carbon monoxide poisoning it can take several hours to flush the gas completely from the human system. I was also unsure of the effect of the extreme cold air we were breathing, which would not only be slowing down our circulation, but could also be affecting our respiratory system and oxygen gas exchange. I had my first moment of panic as my *gut* heaved.

What were we doing in this inhospitable climate gasping for our lives?? Not a good start to the expedition.

Happily we all slowly began to recover. I was keen, as soon as I could get my wits about me, to keep us all moving. Hypothermia and frostbite on top of Co_2 poisoning was by then dawning on me as being a distinct possibility.

Happily over the next 30 minutes, apart from cracking headaches, we all made a rapid recovery. I was still concerned, as to how this was going to, not only affect us over the next few hours, but also how we were going to survive the expedition without being able to warm the tent with our stoves. Surely tent material is designed to let the air in and out?

It soon became obvious what had happened. The heat from the stoves had melted the frozen air particles in the air which had became moist, condensed and frozen against the inner lining of the tent. The stoves were pumping off noxious carbon monoxide which couldn't escape, so the tent soon became a sealed bubble of toxic carbon monoxide fumes that we were all happily inhaling in our quest for warmth! Our tent was now a completely sealed unit as the ice had stopped any normal gas exchange with the air outside through the tent material. We were in fact slowly being poisoned.

The stove was then taken outside and the tent opened right out to let the noxious gas out and clean fresh air in. The canvas was hit to remove the frozen inner ice skin. No one was keen to reenter for a good while. We did, however, soon take cover again as the falling temperatures and wind chill were becoming unbearable. We quickly huddled back inside leaving the stoves outside.

In future when erecting the tent we took care to make sure it was not a sealed unit, and we had some circulating air. We removed the tent floor, and the tent door was now always left wide open as well!

Just spend a moment to imagine sleeping on the sea ice at -40 °C without a tent floor and with the tent flap wide open all night. Yes you're right, it was a tough start to a tough expedition and it was a big wake-up call very early on for us all.

The power of Mother Nature was made obvious to us from very early on in the expedition. This was a beautiful but raw and desolate spot where we felt we were not meant to survive. Man or woman comes to the Arctic by his or her own desires and not by invitation.

Chapter 4
Chainsaw Trauma - Do We Remove Or Not?

"Injuries give you perspective. They teach you to cherish the moments that I might have taken for granted before."
— Ali Krieger

One sunny October morning, I was doing a clinic in a small Family Country Practice. We dealt with most routine minor illnesses and injuries, together with health screening and prevention. As you can imagine, one never quite knew what would come through the door on any given day. We had booked routine appointments, but we also dealt with the unexpected.

Yes, I can feel your trepidation as you embark on this chapter. Imagine my churning *gut* when my receptionist buzzed down to me to let me know that I had an emergency 'walk in'. A tree surgeon with a potentially serious chainsaw injury.

All manner of images came to my mind; however, she did say he was 'a walk in' so I was pretty sure this wasn't a lower limb injury.

I couldn't have been more wrong, as a very pale young man spattered with wood chippings was carefully wheeled into the consulting room.

Gut Feelings

Statistics show that the vast majority of fatal and major injuries in tree work are associated with chainsaw operations. To put this into a wider context, tree work has a major injury incidence rate higher than that of the construction industry.

It seems pretty obvious to state that chainsaws are potentially dangerous machines which can cause major injury if used by inadequately trained people, but they were, and often are, used by unskilled workers, especially during the 1990's when this accident happened. I believe that nowadays people are more safety conscious, and if you use a chainsaw at work you should have received adequate training and be competent in using one for that type of work. *http://www.hse.gov.uk/treework/newto.htm*

The patient arrived in my consulting room accompanied by his also very pale companion. I quickly assessed the presenting situation.

I noticed that he was wearing both his boots, and his legs looked intact, his arms were intact and his face, although extremely pale and filthy, was not injured. He seemed to have all his fingers.

A slow sinking *gut* feeling was dawning on me as I noticed a steady drip of blood from his R boot onto our pristine white treatment room floor.

On closer inspection I could see that his right safety steel capped boot was held on by a dirty rag which was now oozing with a spreading flow of blood.

Chainsaw Trauma - Do We Remove or Not?

My *gut* feeling at this stage as I began to take in the potential severity of the injury was that —— Oops, this was one for our Accident and Emergency Department (ER) and not me. My job at that moment was 'First Aid' till the emergency services arrived. I immediately arranged for an Emergency Blue Light ambulance to attend as I could see the patient was accelerating towards a near collapsed state, with major blood loss and shock.

If I were to remove the boot I would potentially also be removing the foot, which my *gut* instinct told me was a very, very, very, bad idea!

It looked like he'd severed his dorsalis pedis artery which runs over the top of the foot, and by the look of the mangled boot mixed up with torn flesh, he had also possibly done some major damage to his foot, if not a partial amputation.

It transpired that the lad was unskilled and had been working with a friend. They had been privately contracted by a domestic householder to top and trim a tree. He was untrained, using a chain saw he had not used before, and free climbing, cutting as he went. When reaching down to trim a lower branch, the chain saw had kicked back and made contact with his R boot. He was unsure of how bad the injury was, which is why they had come directly to the local Community Health Centre and not to The Accident and Emergency department. He had little feeling in his foot, which was extremely worrying. By the time he arrived he was unable to walk and things felt decidedly unstable in the foot department! He had not removed the boot for fear of what they might find, but instead wrapped it up in a rag they found in their van. The patient was now also suffering from shock and what seemed like a moderately large loss of blood.

On closer examination, the boot and foot were definitely attached to each other but whether or not they were still attached to the ankle and by how much was yet to be discovered. The chainsaw injury looked pretty extensive and the damage probably severe. The impression was that by keeping the boot on and binding it in place had been the best thing they could have done at the time. My job at this time was to treat his shock and replace fluids as I had no idea how much blood had been lost.

Happily the emergency service were with us promptly and he was hastily whisked off to the Emergency Department, while I telephoned ahead to the orthopedic surgeons to meet him there.

On further contact with the patient later that week, I discovered that he had indeed almost amputated his foot. Leaving the boot on was apparently one of the reasons that they were able to save his foot! He underwent extensive surgery with internal fixation and although now sporting a large scar, he made an almost full recovery. There was some bone and soft tissue tendon damage, which took a good while to repair. He has unfortunately been left with loss of feeling and numbness on the top of his foot and toes. He finds this is only a problem if he injures his foot, as he tends not to notice any pain at the time of injury.

Arboriculture is highly skilled job and those carrying out the work should be fully trained and competent. This would help prevent accidents like this one occurring.

The work at the clinic was never without its surprises, and one was often left wondering at the fragility of our human bodies and the fine line between a fully operational unit and complete disaster.

Chapter 5
Arctic Blizzard - Mission Medical Log ... 'Critical'

"It takes determination to see a dream come to pass. The question is not will you start, but will you finish."
— Joel Osteen

By this part of the expedition to the Geomagnetic North Pole, we were nearing The Sverdrup Pass, also known as Polar Bear Pass. It passes through a gap in the glaciers of Eastern Ellesmere Island, and is an ancient route used by the Inuits hunting this area when the weather is significantly warmer. It was originally established to protect a key travel route for polar bears and Inuits during the spring and summer. This was to be our route and a challenging leg of our journey. This area is very remote, with unpredictable weather and frequent rock and snow falls which often block the pass. The start of the pass was a deep canyon which once you started down was difficult to exit in a hurry. It was also an area where for at least 10 days we would not be able to get rescued should things go wrong . The canyon was almost impossible to climb out of, and there was absolutely nowhere for a sea plane, with skis, to land. The passage was narrow and also a pass that polar bears use. There were steep rock and snow falls to negotiate and clamber over and around. The route was around 80 km long and wound round and up and down with many twists and turns, so you never knew if a polar bear was around the next corner!

Polar bears, being almost completely unused to the presence of humans, have no ingrained fear of people. Their aim is to hunt for food and if a human happens to appear unexpectedly in their path then that's naturally a nice tasty snack, thank you. We were as prepared as possible for this event, and with the right precautions, polar bears are easily deterred.

This didn't, however, allow us to put our guard down, so we were always on full alert to the distinct possibility of an encounter. We did have quite a serious polar bear encounter earlier on during the expedition so we were well prepared.

A few days before the start of the pass, the weather suddenly took a turn for the worse and we found ourselves battling against ever increasing severe blizzard conditions and bone-numbing wind chill. Under difficult, near blinding conditions, we eventually managed to get the tent up and gratefully took refuge from the stinging frozen assault. The wind continued to howl outside like screaming banshees for 3 days non-stop. Mother Nature was calling a stop to the expedition for at least a day or so. The severe blizzard virtually buried our tent.

We settled down to sit out the storm and gain some much needed rest.

Over the last few days one of the team had developed a nasty blister over his entire heel. I had been dealing with blisters, bruising, frostbite and other expedition injuries on a daily basis and we seemed to be keeping on top of most things. The temperature had not risen much above -30 °C on the expedition, and as a result we were all suffering from frostnip to our extremities, and frost bite to our fingertips was pretty widespread.

I was also suffering from some frostbite damage to my nose, especially my nasal septum. The very fact that I was continually inhaling freezing air and exhaling warm air was causing frostbite to the cartilage dividing the two nostrils. When I later needed surgery on this, my bemused ENT surgeon said he normally did nasal septum repairs for cocaine drug addicts and I was the first, and probably last, explorer he would do this procedure on.

I digress; that evening when I did my evening health checks on the team, the large heel blister was causing some concern. I had left the skin intact to prevent infection entering. I was dressing it daily and had been keeping a good eye on it, but that evening when I enquired how it felt, I was informed that it no longer hurt when he walked and in fact he couldn't feel his heel at all. I was immediately alerted that all was not well. With a sinking *gut* feeling, I examined the blister which covered his entire heel. It was hard and cold and a very dark colour. It slowly dawned on me that the liquid in the blister had frozen and he was now suffering from frostbite to his heel! This was a serious complication and in retrospect, I should have considered this possibility. I could no longer leave this intact as more damage could result. I also needed to ascertain how bad the frost bite was and how deep it had gone.

I decided to excise the area, drain the blister and see what damage there was to the surrounding tissue.

On further examination, once I had drained the blister, I noted some dead black necrotic tissue covering the entire heel. To allow healthy tissue to survive I needed to take this sloughy dead necrotic tissue back to healthy tissue with a scalpel. As the tissue was dead, my patient experienced little discomfort. He was also unable to see what I was doing! Happily the surrounding tissue looked healthy, well perfused and was not showing any signs of infection.

My duty now was to dress the wound, keep it as clean as possible, and start prophylactic antibiotics as there was every possibility that this wound would now get infected. We had gone from frozen microbes to the very real possibility of warm multiplying ones! This was potentially a medevac situation.

Sadly Mother Nature had other ideas. No decision was needed as there was no possibility of help. Our severe weather, with blizzards and driving snow, had not only cut us off from the outside world, but prevented any possible air rescue as the storm continued to rage. It had also cut off all satellite phone contact. The extreme weather prevented the expedition continuing further and there could be no air rescues for a few days or until we could get satellite contact again.

We were truly alone in a small tent with a screaming storm raging outside. There was the worrying possibility that a serious medical emergency could develop should any infection take hold. Having experienced a flesh-eating disease with another explorer the previous year, which needed immediate rescue therapy, the possibility of a similar situation was not far from my mind!

Serendipity played a hand here, as this storm gave my patient the much needed rest and elevation that the affected limb really appreciated and needed.

I was, however, still prepared to get him Medevaced out as soon as we could get radio contact again. To walk on this heel and continue the journey would be almost impossible with such a large open wound.

We were all well aware that the next leg of our journey was Polar Bear Pass and no air lift would be possible for many days, once we'd set off down this impenetrable canyon.

At this point, as the medic on the team, it was my duty to advise that the safest most sensible action was to get him air rescued once we got radio satellite contact again. This was not what he wanted. He was quite determined to continue and asked me please to keep dressing his heal to allow him to do this. By this time we were well into the expedition and had overcome so many obstacles. He stressed that we had come so far, and conquered so much, it was inconceivable for him to give up now.

Medically my advice, as I was at pains to elaborate on, was not only the reality of his demise should his heel become infected, but also that his decision could jeopardise the entire expedition should he worsen. Not to mention the pain he would experience when trying to walk with this injury.

My *gut* feeling was that, having experienced his tenacity during the expedition so far, this guy was made of tough *guts*! He had responded well to his treatment regime and was quite determined to carry on. Deep down I knew he could make it, come what may, and I was prepared to help him as best I could.

He duly signed a waiver and Polar Bear Pass welcomed our intrepid team for the next stage of our adventure.

Chapter 6
Psychotic Attack - Never Turn Your Back!

> *"Someone who smiles too much with you can sometimes frown too much with you at your back."*
> — Michael Bassey Johnson

Caring for those with mental health issues has changed radically over the last 30 years. This shift in caring for people with mental health problems in psychiatric institutions to caring for them in the community was called deinstitutionalisation. It is recorded that there were around 100,000 people in institutions before the change and now these asylums are all closed. The change was driven by a growing emphasis on human rights. There were some key issues that workforce planning had to address when considering caring for all these patients in the community. This all started with asylums reducing admissions in the 60's; however, it did not fully take off until the late 80's when they started closing these institutions on mass. As a result the community took on a lot of the care that had previously been done in an institutional setting. The GP community surgeries at that time had a subsequent increased caseload when taking on the care of some of these patients. Evidence now suggests that there were shortcomings in this deinstitutionalisation, with the failure to engage and consider the role of primary care practitioners. Some see that this has had a negative impact on subsequent provisioning.

At the surgery where I was working at the time, we would regularly see patients with mental health issues who needed their antipsychotic depot injections. These appointments were generally slotted in during normal busy routine clinics and in most cases didn't cause any issues. On one occasion, however, I had called in a patient who I had seen on a regular basis over the last few months. He was managing well in the community and was well supported by his family and a good mental health team. He routinely came to the health clinic for his regular depot injections.

A depot injection deposits a drug in a localised mass, called a depot, from which it is gradually absorbed by the surrounding tissue. Such injections allows the active compound to be released in a consistent way over a long period. This method of medication is used routinely with patients with mental health issues, and allows them to have a consistent dose to keep them mentally stable so they can live safely in the community setting.

It had been noted that this patient had missed an appointment. He was reminded to attend on numerous occasions, and eventually he agreed to attend for his injection. On this occasion he seemed more animated than usual, was smiling a lot, and said he was feeling much better not being on his medication and was considering stopping it. I discussed this with him and he agreed to have a review to discuss this further with the psychiatrist team he was under at this time. He was compliant and willing, and agreed to have the injection today, but he wanted to delay any further injections until he had had an update with his mental health team. He mentioned that he still occasionally heard voices; however, as long as he did as he was told, he felt he was able to manage this. I was slightly concerned by this and made a note to contact his mental health team following his visit.

The clinic room I was working in that day had recently been changed around so that the examination couch was accessible from both sides for easy examination of a patient on the couch and not up against the wall, as it had previously been. This also meant that there was no easy exit from the room, from the other side of the couch, should the need arise.

The patient in question sat waiting quietly in a chair by the door as I drew up his injection on the other side of the couch. I did have most of my back to him, although I could still see him out of the corner of my eye. I was busy concentrating, however, on the matter at hand of drawing up the medication in a syringe.

In a flash, I had a *gut* feeling that things were about to get messy, and I was in danger. The atmosphere in the room changed markedly and on *gut* instinct I pressed the panic button. My patient had drawn a knife and his intention was clear. I had no way of escaping around the examination couch to the door. This knife looked big and menacing, and the patient was intent on using it. He was swinging it haphazardly around as I tried to avoid it, sweating profusely. I prayed

1. That the panic button worked, as I had never used it before.
2. That someone would hear it.

Gut Feelings

What a relief when one of my colleagues burst through the door with the emergency resuscitation trolley, thinking I had activated the button because of a cardiac arrest. The trolley, luckily, firmly knocked my attacker off his guard and we soon had the situation back under control. The patient was restrained, medicated and taken to a safe place for all concerned.

After recovering from the ordeal, I spent a good few minutes firmly chastising myself for my complete lack of insensitivity to the potential danger I had put myself under. My mental health training had mainly involved caring for patients on geriatric psychiatric ward at the Eastern Hospital in Hackney London in the 1970's! They were mostly bed bound and if a danger to themselves or each other, heavily medicated or restrained. They had spent most of their lives in institutions before the deinstitutionalisation had taken place.

You will be interested to hear that the clinic room was subsequently returned to its former arrangement and the adjoining door was in future always left open during such consultations. It has since been recognised that the impact of caring for mental health patients in the community has had a negative impact in a few areas. The UK Royal College of General Practitioners is aware of this and acknowledges that mental health problems in primary care are common, and that the range of mental health problems encountered by a GP is large. A recent report by the Parliamentary and Health Service Ombudsman states that patients with mental health conditions and their families are suffering needless distress and are being badly let down by the National Health Service.

Chapter 7
Flesh-eating Disease - 1575 MEDEVAC Miles Away

> *"Don't speak ill of your predecessors or successors.*
> *You didn't walk in their shoes."*
> — Donald Rumsfeld

As the expedition medic on a polar research mission, I was responsible for my team of 6 others intrepid nutters. It was our first year in the high Arctic and we were gathering data on how the body coped with extreme conditions in this inclement world of sea ice, with temperatures down to -40 °C and unnatural light conditions. My job was not only to collect blood samples and body fluids but also to keep the team healthy and manage any sickness or injury. I knew I was a long way away from any proper medical backup, should I have a medical emergency. On good days, when the weather was clear, a medevac from Iqaluit (our nearest medical center), was 1,575 kilometres to the south. A medical team can arrive in Resolute about six hours after it's summoned in good conditions to rush urgent-care cases to surgery. On rough days, however, the time it takes to fly a patient to Iqaluit, or farther south, is anybody's guess. If the weather is inclement with blizzard conditions, it is often impossible for a medical team to arrive for days on end.

I was trained in managing emergencies at expedition level, and the whole team had advanced first aid training prior to the expedition. I can clearly remember our tutor warning us that we might well have loss of life during this expedition and to deal with this prospect. This brought it home to us all, the dangers we might well be facing, exploring the high Arctic at our own risk, and the lack of medical support in an extreme emergency.

On arriving in Resolute, the team acclimatised by setting out on longer and longer expeditions across the sea ice while collecting samples and data that were duly flown back to the United Kingdom. Taking blood samples at - 30 °C in the field was a challenge to say the least, as the peripheral circulation shuts down when cold. One day on return to base camp, I was dealing with the day's run of blisters, early frost nip and various other minor injuries, when one of my worst nightmares began to materialise before my very eyes!

One of the team had developed a blister on his heal from ill-fitting boots. He had then borrowed a pair of one the locals' boots which had been left behind at the camp we were staying in. Unbeknownst to us, the previous owner of these boots was no longer alive. If we had known this, perhaps things would not have turned out as they did.

I had been treating the blister with a topical antiseptic cream and a dry dressing.

On day two I checked the heel, which was reportedly now becoming incredibly painful. On examination I was overcome by a deep *gut* feeling that all was not well! I was surprised to find

Flesh-eating Disease - 1575 MEDEVAC Miles Away

the blister looking decidedly odd and filled with what looked like an unusually deep red fluid. There was also a purplish rash which fascinatingly seemed to be spreading up from the blister before my very eyes. My patient was also complaining of flu-like symptoms and an incredible thirst. My *gut* feeling was that this was not a simple blister with a mild spreading erythema, but could possibly be an extremely serious flesh-eating disease called necrotising fasciitis.

As a student at St Bartholomew's Hospital in London, I had spent many hours studying in the hospital's wonderful library and had been fascinated by pictures of skin complaints including this flesh-eating disease. These pictures were emblazoned on my mind and it slowly dawned on me that this presentation fitted the picture I saw before me, exactly! I felt sick with apprehension.

The infection is commonly caused by a bacterial infection usually from a group A Streptococcus bacteria. Treatment is usually by an intravenous cocktail of antibiotics. The infection is often an extremely strong variety causing a life-threatening disease and is known as a flesh-eating bacteria. It can also be caused by a mixture of bacteria.

This bacteria destroys soft tissue and is often coupled with toxic shock syndrome-both are deadly!

The bacteria enters the body through an opening in the skin as small as a paper cut or pin prick or as in our case, through weakened skin like a bruise or a blister.

Gut Feelings

The symptoms, including pain around the area and flu-like symptoms together with an intense thirst. These were all present in my patient.

If untreated, within three days the area of body might begin to swell and show a purplish rash. A blister filled with a black fluid might appear and the wound might appear bluish, white or with a dark mottled, flaky appearance.

Eventually if not caught, the body will begin to go into toxic shock from the toxins the bacteria is giving off, and death can occur.
(Information source: National Necrotizing Fasciitis Foundation)

There was a Medical Out Post in Resolute, run by an extremely proficient nurse, so we hurriedly got the patient over there. The nurse agreed that this looked very suspicious and informed us that the far north of Canada, where we were at this time, had recently experienced a number of similar cases with a mortality rate of 30 per cent. One of the cases had been from Resolute and the patient had unfortunately died.

We immediately consulted with the medical team in Iqaluit, 1,500 miles away, and they agreed this did indeed seem to have a suspiciously similar presentation. It was decided that an aggressive treatment of antibiotics administered intravenously was necessary as there was a strong possibility of Necrotizing Fasciitis which eats away the flesh and can quickly prove fatal if left untreated.

Antibiotics were duly administered by intravenous therapy and happily, after a few days on a cocktail of antibiotics, the patient made a good recovery and vowed never to wear a dead man's boots again.

On discussing the case further, it began to dawn on us that the boots that had been borrowed had previously belonged to the deceased man. It seems that this unfortunate gentleman had apparently died the previous year following contracting this flesh-eating disease.

The boots were duly burned.

Chapter 8
Her Dazzle -
Just Naturally with Gravity

Her Dazzle - Just Naturally with Gravity

"A girl can dazzle - just naturally!"
— Paris Hilton

It was late one morning at the end of a busy community family health clinic and my next patient shuffled in. When I say shuffle, I mean, literally shuffled in. I could feel from her reluctance to sit down that something was bothering her deep down. This was going to be a tough one; I could feel it in my *guts*.

I stood also, as to sit down at this point would put her in obvious discomfort on a yet unknown level. I believe she couldn't or didn't want to sit down. So I conducted the consultation at her level with as much empathy as I felt this case needed. Bucket load by all accounts. She told me it had taken her great courage to see me today and she was not even sure that she could follow this through.

We chatted about the inclement weather, a good go-to with the English, as our weather is always changeable and a good topic of conversation.

I invited her to let me know what had brought her to see me today.

Gut Feelings

I was bemused by what she then announced.

"You see, I've grown a dazzle and I'm not sure what to do about it!"

I tried not to look surprised and encouraged further dialogue to ascertain what in fact was going on. My mind meanwhile searched madly through any previous medical presentation to come up with what a dazzle could possibly be.

"Well", she said, "my husband and I have had a very happy marriage and have 3 children and 8 grandchildren. We've always been.........."

she clams up for a while but soon continues, as I keep a straight open face. It's beginning to dawn on me where we are going!

"We've had a good sex life and always called my husband's .... hmmmmm she says.......... his thingy ....well, we've always called it 'his dazzle.' Bless her, she then continued to say, "because he's always dazzled me with it."

Ok, so now we're getting somewhere. She goes on to report that over the last few weeks, she's noticed that she thinks she might be growing her own dazzle. This morning, however, she woke and to her amazement she was sporting the full member!

I was trying so hard to nod and keep my face clinical and formal and stern and just not show any emotion. She was quite serious that she believed she had grown her own dazzle.

On examination she did indeed look like she had her own new member. When the vaginal vault completely descends, it can look remarkably like a man's penis. I was able to quickly reassure her that this was a prolapse of her vagina and nothing for her to worry about as it could be sorted.

The symptoms she had been complaining of, like something coming down, are a common feeling of the muscles in the vagina losing their tone. Other symptoms commonly reported are of a dragging feeling and pressure in the vagina or pelvis, painful intercourse (dyspareunia), a mass at the opening of the vagina and repeated urinary tract infections. Often patients also report a decrease in pain or pressure when the woman lies down.

These prolapses present in varying degrees of severity and are quite common. Though this was the first time I had seen a complete inversion.

A vaginal prolapse occurs when the weight-bearing or stabilising structures that keep the vagina in place weaken or deteriorate. This is the result of damage to the network of muscles supporting the vagina and surrounding tissues and organs. When parts of this support network are weakened or damaged, by childbirth, menopause, surgery or being overweight, the vagina and surrounding structures may lose some or all of the support that holds them in place.

My lovely lady was proud to inform me that she had had three big bouncing boys and was now post menopausal. I explained to her that because of this the muscles had weakened and as a result her vagina had descended. This was not only due to the probable damage during childbirth, but I also explained that after her menopause her oestrogen levels had dropped. This hormone helps to keep the muscles and tissues of the pelvic support structures strong. After menopause, the oestrogen level declines; and the support structures may weaken.

She was very relieved by this explanation and was keen to get the appropriate treatment ASAP.

She explained that her darling husband was keen to deploy his dazzle again and would be relieved that her recent denial on the bedroom front would soon be a thing of the past.

One happy and reassured lady almost skipped out of the surgery and I was left contemplating another of those dazzling experiences I was honoured to being part of, and one I will never forget; it makes me smile to this day.

Chapter 9
Maggots and Spiders
- Wildlife in Unexpected Places!
(*Wildlife in General Practice*)

"The smaller the creature, the bolder the spirit."
— Suzy Kassem

Part 1: Maggot therapy
And a different type of gut reaction

It was a normal Monday morning and my clinic caseload was manageable. The usual post weekend presentations, like sore throats, bumps and bruises, results from previous laboratory, X-ray and scan procedures to discuss, tests to order, referrals to make and so on.

As my morning came to an end, my last case (luckily, as it turned out), was an elderly gentleman who was booked in with a chronic long-term leg ulcer which we had failed to heal after many years of dressing and various treatments. He had been away on holiday for 3 weeks and had not had any dressings done while he was away. It had been hot during this period and he'd been outside in a deck chair, enjoying the fresh air and sunshine. He admitted that he'd taken the dressings off to let the air get to his leg. He said his grandmother was always of the opinion that letting the air to a wound helped it heal. He thought he'd give it a go! He'd had it dressed a week ago however and hadn't touched the dressing since. He had returned from holiday yesterday had come to me today so I could assess his leg as he felt it was irritating quite a lot.

I gloved up and took down the dressing without much thought about what I might find. As I unwound the various layers of bandages and dressings, I noticed that small bits of what I thought were cotton wool began falling to the floor. In my peripheral vision I began to notice that these bits of cotton wool were moving!

Gut reaction - oh yes sireeeeeeee ! I leapt up before I could control myself.

The dressing was heaving with maggots! I believe the patient would have jumped up as well, but he was rather attached to the offending limb. There was also an interesting smell slowly diffusing from the dressing. It can only be described as a sickly sweet *gut* disturbing odour!

Once we'd calmed down (both the patient and I) and reassessed the situation, with permission from the patient, other clinical members of the surgery were summoned to witness this interesting event that was unfolding in the treatment room.

As I removed the last heavily infested bandage, to our amazement, the actual leg ulcer was super clean with no dead necrotic tissue and wonderful healthy, new granulation tissue now spreading over the entire area.

There was no smell from the leg which looked pink and healthy; however, the smelly moving bandages were duly double yellow bagged and disposed of.

There was great interest in this phenomenon from all attending, and it certainly triggered some further research.

I'm pleased to report that the leg continued to heal and within a few weeks he was off our books. The condition resolved within a couple of weeks naturally following the maggot therapy. The years of regular dressings using the best, up to date, well researched, very expensive, lotions, potions and dressing just had not worked Was his grandmother right in her old wives tale?

Isn't it marvelous what nature can do when given the opportunity?

I'm not advocating doing this yourself; however, medical research does show that using maggots to clean a wound has some success. Maggots are used today, not only on non-healing necrotic skin and venous stasis ulcers but also soft tissue wounds, pressure ulcers, neuropathic foot ulcers, non-healing traumatic and post-surgical wounds, with some success.

To quote - *https://en.m.wikipedia.org/wiki/Maggot_therapy*

'Maggot therapy is a type of biotherapy involving the introduction of live, disinfected maggots (fly larvae) into the non-healing skin and soft tissue wound(s) of a human or animal for the purpose of cleaning out the necrotic (dead) tissue within a wound (debridement) and disinfection'.

"The mind cannot support moral chaos for long. Men are under as strong a compulsion to invent an ethical setting for their behavior as spiders are to weave themselves webs." John — Dos Passos

Part 2: Arachnophobia
Another, different kind of *gut* reaction!

The other case causing, again, a different sort of *gut* reaction was the unexpected encounter with an arachnid.

A patient was booked in to see me with a recent history of the sudden onset of tinnitus. Tinnitus is the term used for a noise in the ear like a ringing, clicking, hissing or sometimes roaring, when there is no similar external sound present.

On taking a full history from this particular patient, it became clear that this was a rather strange case of tinnitus which didn't fit the diagnostic criteria. The worst symptoms where at night, in which she described the noise as a loud tapping or clicking sound, which was deafening and causing sleep disturbance. She also mentioned an irritation in her ear canal and wondered if she might have an infection.

I fully examined the patient and found no other anomaly apart from her noisy, irritating ear.

I must explain here that we use an auroscope for examining the internal auditory (ear) canal and tympanic membrane (ear drum). This piece of equipment has a magnification of typically around 8 diopters (3.00xMag), so any anomaly can be assessed clearly under such magnification. Therefore something small will look extremely large when observed through an auroscope.

I carefully examined her good ear to find it healthy. I then placed the auriscope into her offending ear. I was not expecting to see what looked (under high magnification) like a large tarantula spread out across her ear drum! My *gut* reactions took over, I'm afraid, and I let out a loud exclamation! In my shock I also dropped my auroscope. I muffled my scream as best I could in the circumstances by a coughing and spluttering an apology. I've never been very good with spiders, having lived in Africa as a child. We were taught at a young age to show an extreme respect for anything resembling the 8 legged variety, as some spiders in Africa can be extremely dangerous if crossed!

The commotion I made naturally alerted my colleagues next door (door open between treatment rooms now, see chapter 5) who came rushing in to my rescue, presuming that I was under attack again.

Maggots and Spiders - Wildlife in Unexpected Places!

My poor patient was sweating by now at my obvious shock. I was soon in charge of my breathing and apologised, reassuring my patient and my colleagues that what I had discovered on examination was totally resolvable and an ear syringing would sort the issue with out directly.

I mumbled incoherently about a foreign body and shot next door to gather the equipment for an immediate and gentle ear syringing of the offending foreign body.

The subsequent ear washout demonstrated a very, very, very small money spider that had taken up residence in my patient's comfortable warm auditory canal and had been spinning a very fine web, which I unfortunately had to destroy. Said spider was duly released into the sink and I am unable to comment on its life expectancy following the experience.

I was forgiven by my now understandably relieved patient, and unremittingly teased forthwith by my amused colleagues.

Chapter 10
The Little Caribbean Miracle - Spontaneous Healing?

The Little Caribbean Miracle - Spontaneous Healing?

"And now here is my secret, a very simple secret:
It is only with the heart that one can see rightly;
what is essential is invisible to the eye."
— Antoine de Saint-Exupéry, The Little Prince

It was a hot afternoon during a noisy busy cardiac clinic on a little Caribbean island in the West Indies when a little miracle was brought in.

These cardiac clinics are held twice a year and are run and funded by volunteers. They are an opportunity for local children who have been born with heart problems to get free assessment and treatment. Two cardiologists and a sonographer give up their time to fly in. Local nurses and doctors help with the clinics. I was honoured to be part of this amazing team.

This wonderful story is about a little Caribbean miracle called Alesha (not her real name) who had been born with an inoperable heart defect. At birth a murmur was noted and she showed signs of failing to thrive. She had trouble feeding, was not growing or gaining weight as expected, and was a poor colour throughout, but especially around her lips. She had a referral from her doctor to the clinic as she was obviously in some sort of heart failure.

Gut Feelings

During the consultation the sonography picked up a large inoperable heart defect which would eventually result in the inability of her heart to supply oxygenated blood to her body which would gradually weaken. Her family were aware there was little that could be done and it was now up to them to make her life as happy and comfortable as possible.

The family accepted this diagnosis with meekness and strength of spirit I had seldom seen. The father told me that they had a strong faith and it was up to God to care for them all now and they would leave it in his hands. They refused any form of medication as they were aware that there was little any pharmaceutical drug could do.

As they left I felt an odd *gut* feeling that we would see them again. All of them!

We were a little surprised, however, to see the family again 6 months later. We had truly believed this little bundle would struggle to survive.

As they walked in my heart and *gut* did a somersault - talk about *gut* feelings! They were carrying a little person who looked like any other healthy 9-month-old baby!

How could this be?

Had they swapped the child?

The Little Caribbean Miracle - Spontaneous Healing?

Had there been a twin we didn't know about?

The bemused cardiologist checked her over and the sonography showed pictures of what seemed to be a normal heart with no signs of a defect!

We compared the before and after pictures again and again with amazement and I have to say, with some bemusement. We were bewildered, but all we could do was document her spontaneous remission.

We were left wondering .....
What was this?
What had happened?
Is this possible?
Had we missed something ?
Had we got the names mixed up?
So many questions ...

The family were smiling and looking calm and accepting of our bemusement. The father volunteered that there was no need to tell them; they knew it was good news. Needless to say, there were tears all around.

The father went on to tell me that after their previous appointment when they had been given the bad news, they had gone home and called the whole family and their priest together and asked for their prayers. They truly, truly believed this miracle was directly a result of their combined prayers and their total faith in the divine. They were radiating happiness and I can say it was quite contagious.

Some will call this a spontaneous healing and on researching further, this is indeed a known phenomenon. I personally have never seen anything like this and even today I still wonder if there was some sort of mix-up which we missed.

An authority on this is Dr Andrew Weil, who travelled extensively around the world collecting stories about similar incidents. He describes spontaneous healing not as a miracle but a fact of biology ... the natural healing system we are all born with.

I'll leave you to come to your own opinion on this little miracle.

As far as I'm aware, the child continues to thrive and I continue to be honoured to have been part of such a wonderful experience.

> ***The future belongs to those***
> ***who believe in the beauty of their dreams.***
> — Eleanor Roosevelt

About the Author

Dr Fizzy is from the UK and is a board certified, integrated medical doctor, licensed acupuncturist, advanced nurse practitioner and is a married mother of three. Her interests focus on what makes our bodies function optimally.

She has a lifetime of experience working in the UK as a clinician, in hospitals, GP surgeries, travel medicine and out of hours urgent care.

She was the medic for a North Pole expedition, and also raised funds, and collected data for research, working alongside Cancer Research UK in the the high arctic.

She has also spent time doing humanitarian work in The West Indies, South America and Africa.

Fizzy continues to work in clinical practice and is a research fellow at St George's University Medical School in Grenada.

She is currently circumnavigating the globe by sailing yacht, whilst working between times.

The author is available for delivering keynote presentations on her Arctic Expeditions. For rates and availability please contact the author directly at: gutfeelingsmedic.com

To order more books, please visit:
www.amazon.com

Finally, if you've enjoyed this book, do pass it on, and don't forget to listen to those *gut* feelings; it's your **intuition** (inner you teaching you).

Printed in Great Britain
by Amazon